For my dad, Eugene,
Who, as a child, hid his pajamas to escape bedtime.
And for my mom, Maureen,
Who taught me to love stories. Love you both!

J.H.L.

For my nieces,
Malia, Mary Rachael, Anna Marie, Sariah, Emma, Kailee,
Emily, Isabel, Tysie, Paige, Aryiah, McKenzie, Madilyn
and Mallory—
Spirited fillies one and all.

G.W.B.

ISBN 978-0-9851005-3-7

Printed in China

LazyOne, Inc.
Timbuktu, Madagascar, Bronx
Fargo, Little Rock, Tijuana, Siberia.

This Book Belongs To:

Name: _____

Phone: _____

LAZY one.

Pasture Bedtime

A cautionary tale

By Jenny H. Lyman

Illustrated by Gideon Burnett

Down on Mac's Farm, there lived a young filly
who cantered and frolicked and loved being silly.

Her name was Lil' Anne,
and she played all the day
'Til her mom whinnied loudly,
"Lil' Anne! Hit the hay!"

Then off she would trot
to her snug little stall
And sleep 'neath the moonbeams
that shone through the wall.

Well, one evening as Lil' Anne trotted to bed
She heard her friend Owl flap her wings overhead.

"Lil' Anne!" the owl hooted, "I bid you goodnight!
I'm off to have FUN 'cause I party 'owl' night!"

When the owl flew away,
Lil' Anne just felt mad.
"Why should I go to bed
when there's fun to be had?"

And from that moment on,
Lil' Anne started scheming.
"It's time to stop bedtime and
snoring and dreaming!"

So the very next night, Lil' Anne tried "Plan A."
She buried her jammies deep under the hay.

When Momma neighed "Bedtime!"
Lil' Anne told the mare,
"My jammies are lost—
I have *nothing* to wear."

"I can't go to bed without PJ's!"
she said.
"I'll just *have* to stay up
and keep playing instead."

Well, "Plan A" didn't work.
Momma threw her a blankie.

Lil' Anne hoofed it to bed,
feeling sulky and cranky.

The next day was "Plan B."
Lil' Anne snuck to the shed.

Her new plot involved Rooster,
and here's what she said:

"If you 'cock-a-doodle-doo'
right at dusk, without warning,
we'll fool the whole farmyard—
they'll think that it's morning!"

So when the sun set,
    Rooster crowed with his might!

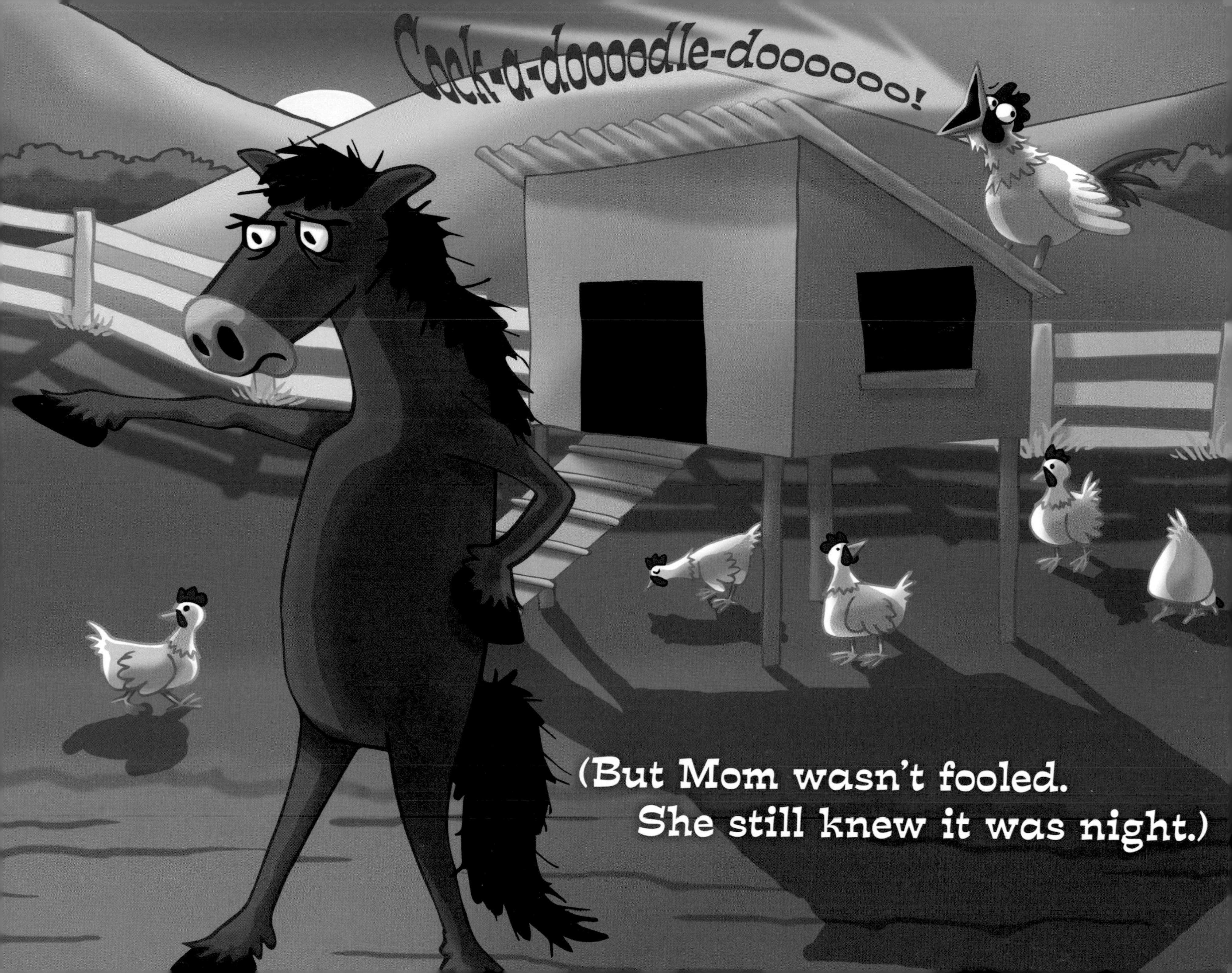

(But Mom wasn't fooled.
She still knew it was night.)

"Plan C" took effect when
Lil' Anne saw the sheep—
the "sheep walkers" who always
walked in their sleep.

When Mom called, "It's bedtime!"
Lil' Anne walked around,
her eyes closed, her arms raised,
two hooves on the ground.

"Okay," Momma sighed.
"Stay up, if you're able.
But be warned: in the morning
you'll feel quite unstable."

So Mom hit the hay, while Lil' Anne just kept playing!
She pranced 'round the pasture, skipping and neighing.

"I'm just like the owl!" Lil' Anne romped and had fun—
but everything changed with the rise of the sun.

Lil' Anne felt SO tired.

And dizzy.

And sick.

Her head hurt.

Her knees shook.

She wanted bed—

QUICK!

See, every young creature
needs sleep to feel good.
So "Plan D" was GO TO BED—
just when she should.

Ever after, at bedtime,
all foals obeyed mommas.
They brushed all their teeth
and put on their pajamas.

And now it's YOUR turn.
It's the end of this rhyme.
Lil' Anne says "Goodnight!"
'cause it's "pasture bedtime!"

Other books with matching pajamas
available from LazyOne:

Duck Duck Moose

Bearly Awake

The Monster Under the Bed